9.00
AUCTION MONEY 10/91

E
GRA

DATE DUE

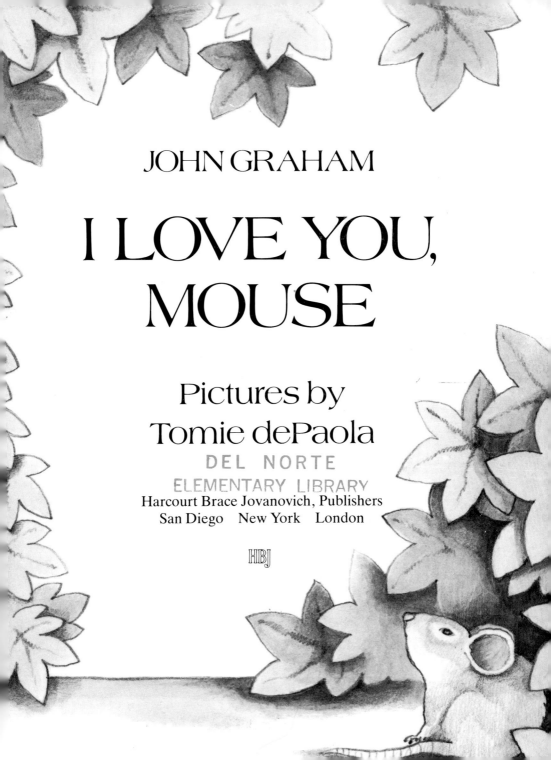

JOHN GRAHAM

I LOVE YOU, MOUSE

Pictures by
Tomie dePaola

Harcourt Brace Jovanovich, Publishers
San Diego   New York   London

HBJ

Library of Congress Cataloging in Publication Data
Graham, John, 1926-
I love you, mouse.
SUMMARY: A child imagines the things he would
do with various animals if he were one of them.
[1. Animals — Fiction] I. De Paola, Thomas Anthony.
II. Title.
PZ7.G7526Iad   [E]   76-8022
ISBN 0-15-238005-1
ISBN 0-15-644106-3 (pbk.)

Printed and bound by
South China Printing Company, Hong Kong

B C D E F
C D E F G (pbk.)

For Sophia Jane, My Mouse

I love you, mouse,

and if I were a mouse,
I'd make you a furry nest.
And we'd curl up together
and nibble some cheese.

I love you, kitten,

and if I were a cat,
I'd make you a soft basket.
And we'd drink warm milk
and stretch ourselves.

I love you, puppy,

and if I were a dog,
I'd build you a kennel.
And we'd play tag
and, sometimes, chase a cat.

I love you, piglet,

and if I were a pig,
I'd build you a sty.
And we'd dig roots
and loaf in the mud.

I love you, chicky,

and if I were a chicken,
I'd build you a coop.
And we'd scratch for corn
and chase a butterfly.

I love you, lamb,

and if I were a sheep,
I'd build you a strong fold.
And we'd graze in the pasture
and grow wool for sweaters.

I love you, cub,

and if I were a bear,
I'd find you a cozy cave.
And we'd hunt for some honey
and watch out for bees.

I love you, tadpole,

and if I were a frog,
I'd find a quiet pond.
And we'd splash in the pond
and have races you'd win.

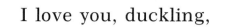
I love you, duckling,

and if I were a duck,
I'd find a blue lake.
And we'd swim all day long
and go "quack-quack."

I love you, gosling,

and if I were a goose,
I'd find a wide marsh.
And we'd play hide-and-seek among cattails
and go "honk-honk."

I love you, bunny,

and if I were a rabbit,
I'd find you a safe burrow.
And we'd play in the moonlight
and eat clover and carrots.

I love you, owlet,

and if I were an owl,
I'd find you a warm tree hole.
And we'd fly together, all night long,
and call out "who-who."

I love you, baby,

and since we're people,

I've built a house for you,

and given you a bed with warm quilts,

a cool drink of water,

a kiss on the nose,

and a quiet good-night.